buckie BOY

A story for the modern underclass

by Ashley Rawson

Acknowledgements

I would like to thank the many people who have aided me in the production of this book, in particular my parents George and Ann Rawson; my brother Jonathan; my nephews Jordan and Matthew and of course my wife and son Jennifer and Thomas. In addition I would like to thank the Glaswegian Ned population who have been a constant source of inspiration throughout this project.

Published by Châteaulait publishing

First published in September 2010 by Châteaulait publishing

Design: Ashley Rawson
Printed and bound by Montgomery Litho Group

ISBN: 978-0-9566702-0-5

www.ashleyrawson.co.uk
ashley@ashleyrawson.co.uk

For Wee Tam and his Mam

Messages In Bottles

The abbey roof was leaking,
Its funds had reached a low,
But then a monk had an idea,
That made its fortunes grow.

"We'll make a tonic wine
To sell throughout the land
And every drink that's purchased
Will be gods cash in hand.

Inside each precious bottle
We'll place a bible text.
Our T.A.M.* will do selection:
Our clients will be blessed!

With sugar, wine and caffeine
Our beverage will sell.
These messages in bottles
Will save lost souls from hell."

And so it came to pass
Upon a sunlit day
That Buckblast Tonic Wine retailed
From Brighton to Strathspey.

Its customers were varied
Although it must be said
That propping up the profits
Was the famous Scottish N.E.D.*

*T.A.M.: Tract Automation Machine
*N.E.D.: Non-Educated Delinquent

The tonic was their rocket fuel;
The bottles they did smash.

The messages they did not read
But rolled for joints of hash.

Daddy Gets Too Wide

Tim's mum died, aged just thirteen
There in Glasgow Town.
So Tam, his teenage daddy,
Passed traditions down:

"If you can smash bus shelters
And dog yer school fur fun
And tag the walls wi menchies
And call the Proddies Huns
And wear a cap and tracky
And smoke spliffs in yer bed
And find yersel a young team
Then... you will be a Ned."

But cruel fate brought a tragedy:
A stolen juggernaut
Ram-raided the off-licence
Where Tam's Buckblast was bought.

The big man was too wide;
Too brave for his own good.
He tried to fight those Billy Boys:
They hit him where he stood.

"The Proddies killed ma Daa," cried Tim.
"They'll never be maa friends.
Ahm gonnae wear maa Celtic strip
And fight them till the end."

In swooped the social services.
Tim cried, "This isnae fair."
An orphaned boy aged only four
Was taken into care.

Driver Under
Instruction

Tiny Tim's First Tipple

Then, one foggy night,
Tim slipped his carers' gaze
And ran with stolen sweeties
To find a hiding place.

And as he munched a bonbon
Behind a bin of trash,
His tiny infant ears
Heard a loud stramash.

Bathed in misty moonlight
A young team drank their wine
Smashing up the swing-park
And committing petty crime.

Police sirens started blaring,
The Neds they scattered fast,
Leaving on a lonely swing
A bottle of Buckblast.

Tim strained to reach the tonic
And downed it like a man,
Then spluttered on a paper note,
Signed, quite simply: 'T.A.M.'

The boy he could not read it
But knew this name too well
"A message from my daddy
In heaven or in hell!"

Proverbs 9:5
"Drink the wine I have mixed"
T.A.M.

Further Neducation

Now Neds shun education,
So few of them can read.
In spite of state resources
Their Neducation breeds.

But little Tim was different:
Not reading made him sad,
As he would miss the messages
In bottles from his dad.

And so he learned his alphabet
And followed his dad's lead
By drinking Buckie in the park
And meeting his own breed.

He found a whole new family -
His neighbourhood young team.
Together they fought boys in blue
Whilst wearing stripy green.

They vandalised their city;
Waged wars at ice cream vans
And battled other young teams
To be the greatest Bams!

Oh what a perfect childhood!
Grafitti, chips and hash.
But as he reached his middle teens
Tim had to make some cash...

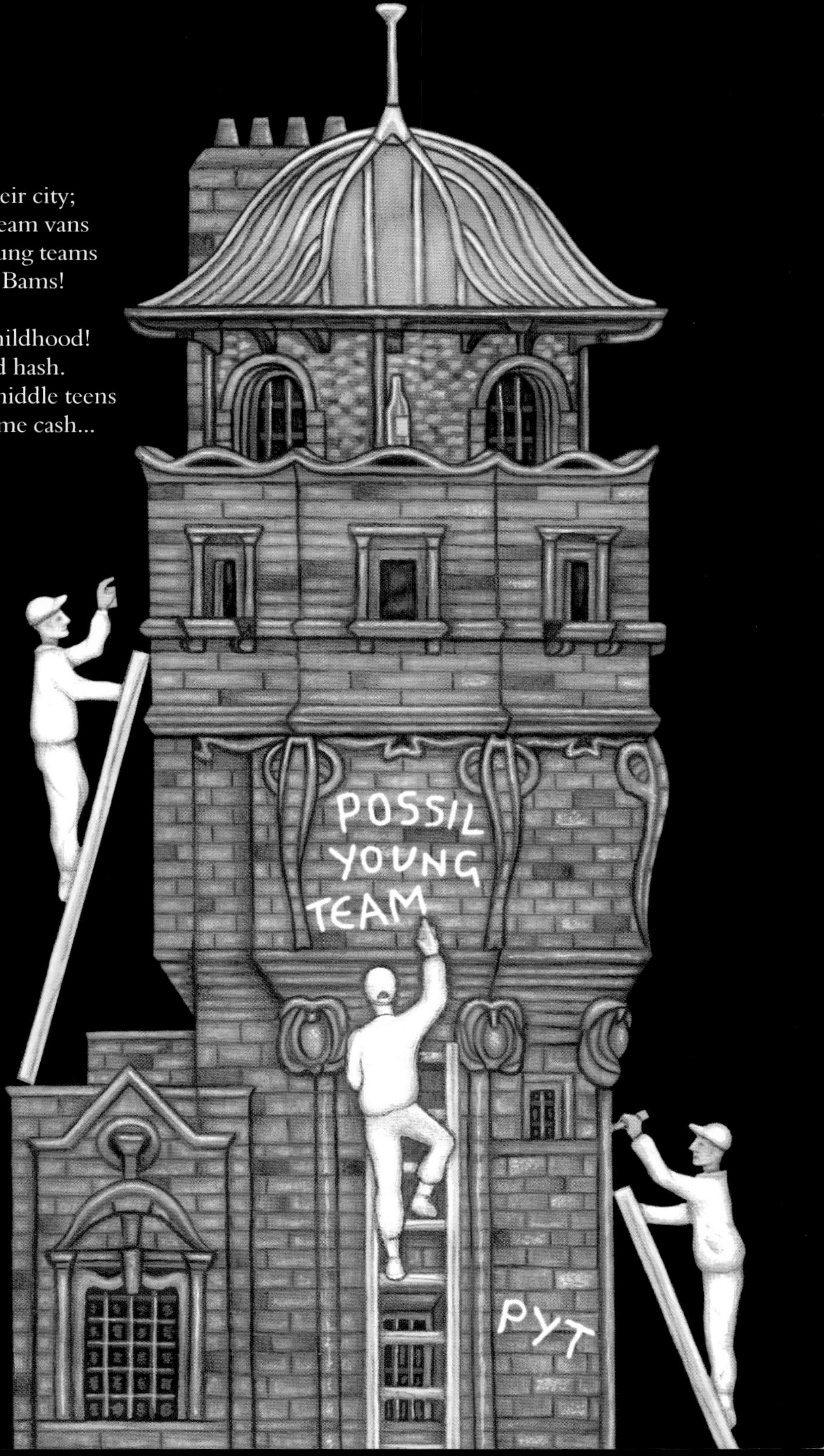

*BAMS: Scottish term short for 'Bampots'
meaning boys of a daft, idiotic nature.

The Statue of Fib-erty

In the city centre
A plinth stood carved in stone.
No statue occupied its base
So Tim made it his own.

Each day he stood upon it
And boomed out a great sound,
"The best deal here in Glesga:
T-shirts fur a poun!"

But Tim was telling fibs:
It was a screen of smoke.
This was a business for the Bams:
He secretly sold dope.

He made a healthy profit-
Until one cold wet day,
Some policemen cordoned off his pitch
And sent him on his way.

"Move along there wee man,
You've had your fun," they said.
"This plinth's for a true idol -
Not a daft wee Ned."

Picking up his Buckie,
Tim poured it down his throat.
"Help me Daa," he whispered,
Before he read his note.

Ezekiel 30:13/14
"...destroy the idols...
and inflict punishment"
T.A.M.

POLICE
POLICE

The Prime Minister

The press pack hummed incessantly:
"They say he's coming round.
He's left the City Chambers.
His car's approaching now!"

A Rolls Royce door swung open.
The P.M.'s feet touched stone.
Then walked towards a cloth-draped shape
Next to a microphone.

"It gives me such great pleasure
This statue to unveil.
Great Donald had a vision
So strong it never failed."

"He fought for Scotland's Parliament
With every single..." THUD!
A headbutt struck the P.M.'s face
And filled his nose with blood.

"Ye nicked maa plinth ya muppet.
Ma Daa says it's nae right."
Tim leapt towards the statue
Continuing the fight.

He scaled the emerald giant
And snapped its specs of green.
Then twenty police manhandled him
And dragged him from the scene.

Revenge of the P.M.

Retreating back to London,
The P.M. read the news
And as his eyes fell on each word
His mouth voiced right wing views.

"That city used to export ships!
Now Neds is all it makes!
Our nation's going to the dogs.
It's time to hit the brakes!

Strewn throughout this island,
Chavvy single mothers
Are turning Britain's children
Into Buckie lovers!

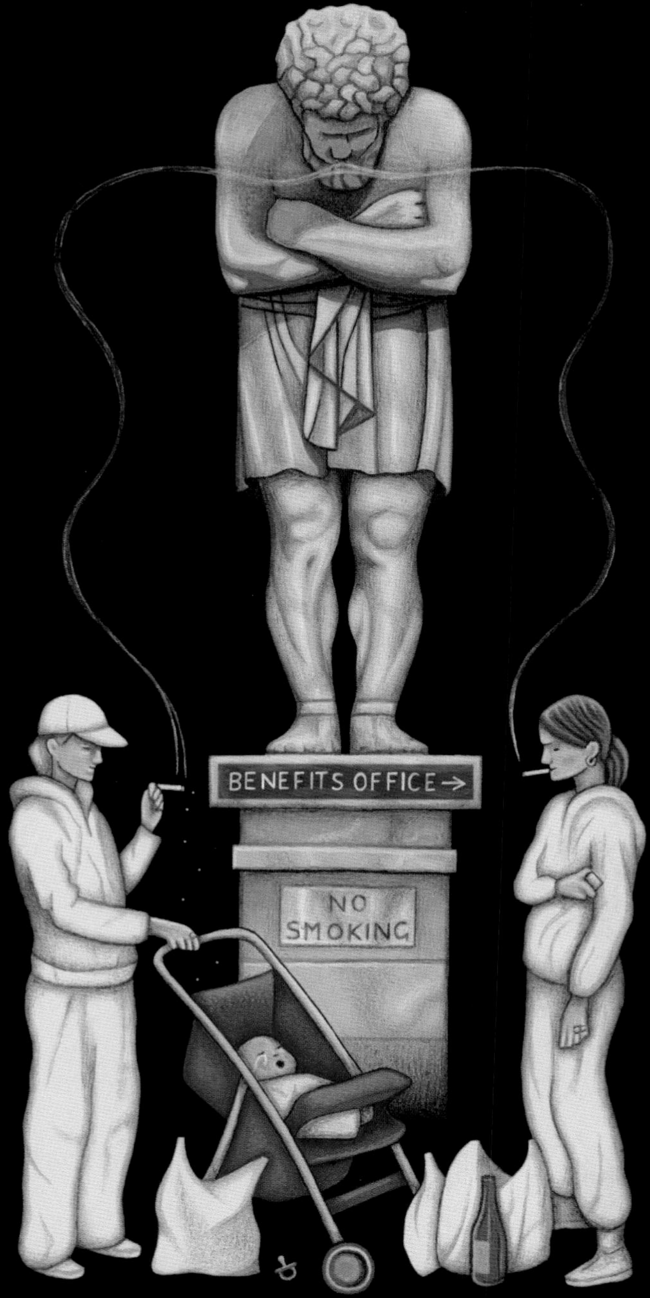

They let their kids run riot,
So by the age of ten
They're drinking booze and having sex...
The cycle starts again!

They live their lives on benefits.
All they do is take!
I'll ban this Buckblast Tonic Wine
For the nation's sake!"

The Drought

Six months on when Tim left jail
He felt sick to the core.
The P.M.'s wrath was in full swing:
His Buckie was no more.

Frustration filled his fevered brow.
"Ah jist can't cope – ah canny!
Let's jist tank oor last Buckies
And go and huv a rammy!"

The night was filled with sirens
As Tim's team reeked revenge.
All they saw they vandalised
To welcome in the end.

Then, as day was breaking
The last bottle was sunk
And cast against a sculpture
Beneath which Tim fell drunk.

He dreamt that his Dad's spirit
Whispered as he lay:
"Ah cannae gee you messages -
The P.M. got his way."

"Daa... ye canny leave me!"
The boy cried in his dream,
"Gonnae jist dae somethin
Fur me and the young team!"

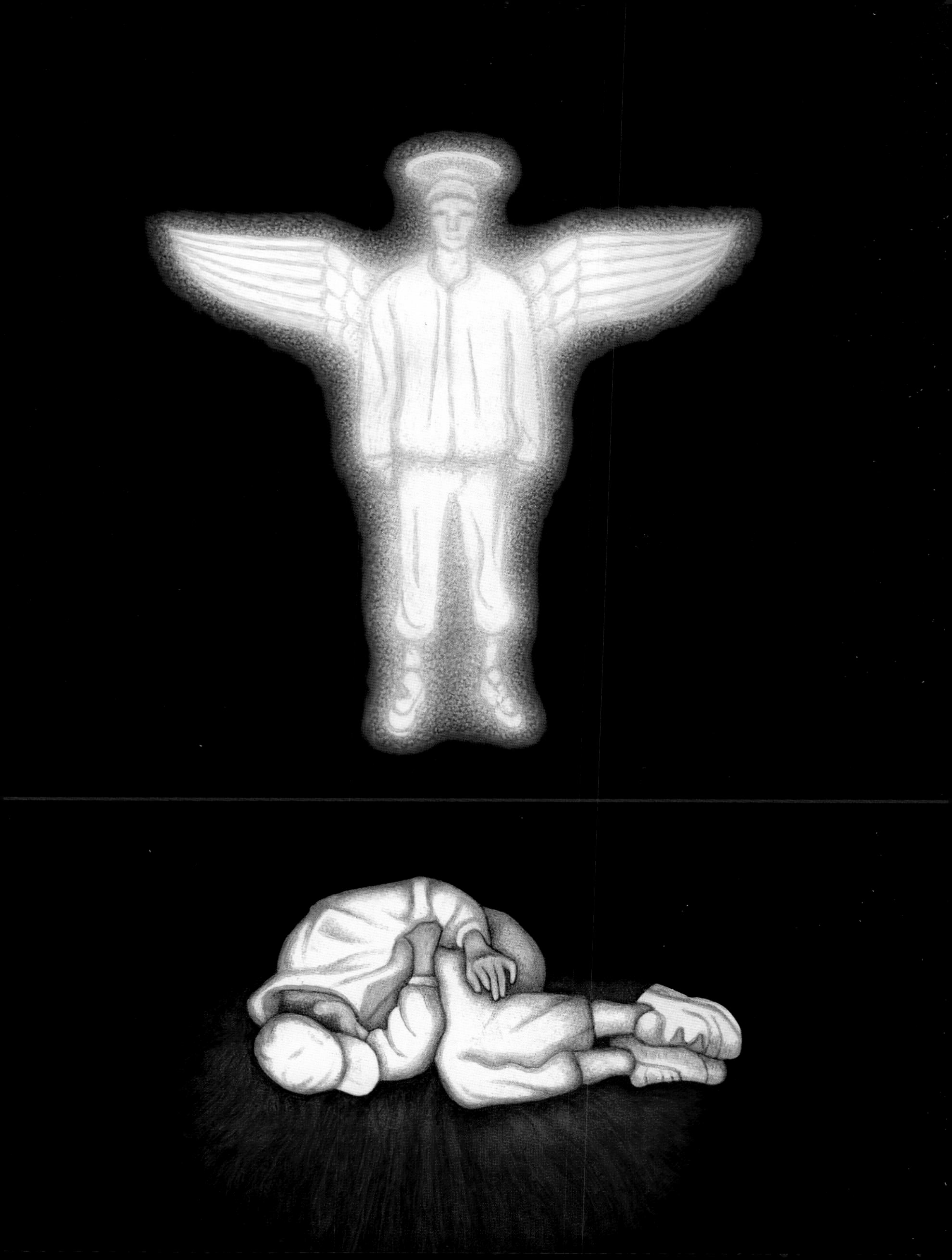

A Miracle

Our hero slumbered sweetly
Till half the day was gone,
There beneath the statue
He broke his bottle on.

Then by the strangest magic
Or maybe God's commands,
Dark drops of ruby liquid
Formed on the sculpture's hands.

A crowd of people gathered.
"Look at that!" they said.
"Blood is flowing from its palms -
Anointing the boy's head."

A priest was duly summoned
To verify the scene.
"Our own Glaswegian miracle –
The greatest ever seen!"

"The boy is clearly chosen
By angels in the sky.
He really should be woken,
My son ...do not be shy."

Tim sat up and licked his lips,
"Oh whit man...Party time!"
It wasn't blood that soaked his face
But Buckblast Tonic Wine!

The young teams flocked from far and wide.
For once they did not fight
But laughed and drank and became friends
Late into the night.

The Buckblast Crusade

Early the next morning
The statue's palms ran dry.
Eight thousand drunken Scottish Neds
Let out a fearsome cry.

They looked to Tim for guidance:
He was their figurehead.
The boy gazed at his Dad's last note:
"Here's maa plan," he said

"The P.M. cannae dae this...
Billys and Tims unite!
We're goin tae march on London.
Oor Buckie is oor right."

They set out early the next day;
Their Sengas joined them too,
And as they headed further south,
The Hoodies swelled their crew.

Then the Spides of Belfast
Crossed the Irish Sea,
And Welsh and English Townie Chavs
Joined their ranks with glee.

Something strange had happened;
A purpose drove them on.
Their social underclass rose up
As thousands became one.

2 Chronicles 20:16
"Tomorrow march down against them"
T.A.M.

The Buckblast Monks heard the news:
"God chose this boy to lead!
We must march on London too!
At once, and with great speed"!

The Big Three

On the third of August
They met at Number Ten:
A monk named brother Osmond,
A Ned, and the P.M.

Two million Bams and thirty monks
Waited in Whitehall.
A nervous silence filled the air
As Tim set out his stall:

"Ye say ye'v bin elected
Ahm here tae rock yer boat:
Me and all maa buddies are
The wans that dinnae vote.

We still live in yer country
And Buckie's oor birthright,
Passed tae us by oor auld Daas
Tae gee oor lives some light.

Yer polis cannae stop us.
Yer army's oan oor side
Even Osmond and the monks
Hink yer bein too wide."

The P.M. snarled, "OK you win!...
Take back your cursed libation!
Drink your Buckie ......have your fill.
Farewell.........my dying nation!"

As they left Ten Downing Street
To a triumphant scene,
Brother Osmond spoke of T.A.M. -
The monks' scripture machine.

"Our messages have worked!
God's moved the country's youth!
They've been directed by his hand!
Young Tim...you are the proof!"

"That's pure mince" retorted Tim.
"Yer talkin like a maddy...
You believe in him upstairs,
And ah'll believe in Daddy."

Full Time

The monks had crates on standby:
The party could begin!
The Bams swarmed to Trafalgar Square
To celebrate their win.

This was their great cup final day
And as wine passed their lips
They did as football players do
And swapped over their strips:

Liverpool with Everton,
Man C with Man U.
Our hero tried to stop himself:
"Ah won't wear proddie blue."

But then a face shone through the crowd
That helped him see the light:
Her chunky earrings dazzled!
Her tan graced skin so white!

The beauty glided to his side:
"Maa name's Versaache Anne.
Ah pure heavy fancy yoo…
Gonnae be maa maan?"

Their young hearts knew it was full time.
Each switched the other's strip
Then sealed their hard fought victory-
With a Glasgow Kiss.

Matthew 22:39
"Love your Neighbour"
T.A.M.

Your Neducation

Ned
Non Educated Delinquent

Neds and other UK Ned cultures

Although the origins of the term 'Ned' are unclear, it has become widely used as an acronym for **'Non Educated Delinquent'**. Neds in their purest form are adolescent Scottish males, of a working class background whose speech, dress sense and behaviour mark them out as a true modern subculture. Female Neds are known as **'Sengas'**. Neds often refer to each other as **'Bams'** or **'Bampots'**: a Scottish word that means daft foolhardy idiot.

Scottish Neds occupy one branch of a broader family tree that has become rooted in UK society. Regional versions of the subculture exist in cities such as Liverpool (**'Scallies'**) and Belfast (**'Spides'**) and in England the word **'Chav'** is used as an umbrella term for all groups exhibiting Neddish characteristics. Additionally the terms **'Townie'** and **'Hoodie'** are commonly used to refer to the subculture.

Ned Fashion

Neds are identifiable by their preference for branded 'trackies' (tracksuits), baseball caps, 'hoodies' (hooded tops) and trainers. These are often combined with football strips, which vary from region to region though many Scottish and Northern Irish Neds wear Rangers or Celtic tops. A further essential fashion accessory is cheap chunky jewellery. Sengas have a particular preference for this and often wear necklaces bearing their names. Sengas also have a passion for peroxide hair, tanning salons and fake tanning products.

Ned Language

Neds have their own dialect that takes the form of a nasal whine punctuated by profanities and inventive word usage. The term *'pure heavy'* is used frequently to add weight to each statement uttered. A full study of Ned linguistics could be the subject of another book but some choice phrases that I have borne witness to are noted below:

"That's pure heavy light maan" ("That really is incredibly light")
Uttered when a Ned friend of mine picked up my new bike to see how heavy it was.

"Ahm pure heavy cheezered" ("I'm really happy")
Witnessed by a teacher friend of mine. A development of the term 'cheesy grin'.

Ned Names

Neds are aspirational in their choice of names for their offspring and often name them after unreachable celebrities, branded clothing or far-flung places. I witnessed my favourite example on a Glasgow bus: a mother with twin daughters called 'Versace' and 'Armani'.

Ned
Non Educated Delinquent (continued)

Neds, Football and Sectarianism
Scottish Neds and Northern Irish Spides are often driven by football related sectarianism that determines whether they align themselves with Glasgow Celtic (Republicanism) or Glasgow Rangers (Unionist). These warped Catholic and Protestant identities (few of them have a true Christian faith) fuel conflict between groups. Gangs of Neds also derive their collective identities from their local areas, forming territorial 'young teams' that fight running battles and engage in petty criminal behaviour.

Football and Sectarian Terms
Below I have detailed the football and sectarian terms used in this book:

Billy Boy:	Protestant Rangers supporter.
Boys in Blue:	Protestant Rangers supporter. Also refers to the police.
Hun:	Protestant Rangers supporter.
Proddie:	Protestant Rangers supporter.
Tim:	Catholic Celtic supporter.

Is Ned culture entirely negative?
No. Many Neds simply add colour to society. Much of the west of Scotland's well known sense of humour is based on Ned antics and linguistics. I have aimed to focus on positives in this book rather than the negative issues of knife crime and violence that are often associated with Ned culture.

Are Neds working class?
Neds, Chavs and the like are often the great grandsons of the true working classes that were employed in heavy industry in the first half of the twentieth century. The Neds of modern UK cities such as Manchester, Liverpool and Glasgow can be seen as the waste product of a post-industrial hangover. No longer required for traditional industrial labour they exist in a state of limbo. A sense of purpose and a steady wage have been replaced by a lack of direction and anti-social behaviour. Not all Neds have a working class heritage however and increasingly middle class Neds are swelling the sub-culture's population.

Neducation
The method by which Ned culture is spread.

Generational Neducation
Many Neds who have a bad diet, drink cheap alcohol, swear, take drugs, carry knives and have sectarian beliefs, are purely following a parental example. From generation to generation Neddish behaviour has been passed down. The education system and state sponsored campaigns aiming to reverse it have continually failed to yield noticeable results.

Neducation
(continued)

The Neducation System
This is the mechanism by which Ned teenagers influence non-Ned classmates, ensuring they take on Neddish characteristics. Essentially it is based on peer pressure and feeds off the natural desire of a child to want to fit in with those around them. Teacher friends of mine have commented on the large numbers of working and middle class boys in their classes who adopt a Neddish nasal whine and unruly behaviour in spite of the presence of a positive teacher and parental influence in their lives.

A direct result of this is that middle class parents have developed a fear of the power of neducation within state secondary schools. Rather than fighting this perceived threat some choose to send their children to private schools instead. Others uproot their families in a bid to place them in the catchment area of a 'better' state school. The schools that are abandoned become increasingly tarnished and children attending them have fewer educated middle class peers to help influence them in a positive direction. In these schools neducation from fellow classmates rather than education from teachers can become the main formative influence on a pupil's life.

Buckblast Crusade

This is a fictional event inspired by two real working class movements from history. The first is the Jarrow Crusade of 1936 when men from Jarrow in Tyne and Wear marched on London protesting against unemployment and seemingly inescapable poverty. The second is the much earlier Chartist movement of 1848 that campaigned for 'a vote for every man' as part of a broader People's Charter. Both of these movements originated from the forefathers of today's working class Neds. This book poses the question: what issue would it take for the modern underclass to rise up and become the political force it once was? A ban on Buckblast Tonic Wine, or something worth fighting for such as true equality of education and class?

Buckblast Tonic Wine

Buckblast or 'Buckie' is a fictional tonic wine made by monks. Any resemblance to a real product is purely coincidental.

Donald Dewar

Donald Dewar was a Labour Party politician who championed the creation of a devolved Scottish Parliament. A statue to his memory was erected in Glasgow's Buchanan Street in 2002. Following several acts of vandalism the statue was given a new six foot tall, Ned-proof plinth in 2005. The illustrations in this book feature the original plinth.

T.A.M.
Tract Automation Machine

T.A.M. is a machine that randomly selects, prints and rolls passages from the Bible. The resulting messages are then placed in bottles of Buckblast Tonic Wine.

Book Illustrations

A Special Thanks

Thank you to anyone who has been entertained enough to purchase one of my prints over the last few years. All sales have helped fund the production of this book. In addition I would like to thank The Glasgow Room (St Enoch Centre, Glasgow), Bob Howie, and Tangent Graphic for their help in promoting my artwork.

Illustrations
in order of appearance

www.ashleyrawson.co.uk
ashley@ashleyrawson.co.uk